FELL BEAUTIES

LEIGHAM SHARDLOW

For my Mum and Dad, Marion and Adam Shardlow. My wonderful wife, Gemma Shardlow, and everyone who has ever believed in me. Thank you so much, from the deepest reaches of my soul.

CONTENTS

EDITOR'S NOTE

A lot of Bizarro concerns itself with the grotesque. The genre lends itself to this, perhaps even defines itself with it. This book not only explores grotesquery as an idea but throws it around, even lets it rain down from the sky. The breakneck cartoon that is Fell Beauties does not shy away from ugliness in any way, to an extent that is impressive even for a Bizarro book. There is a lot of uncomfortable laughter and a lot of cringing ahead but really, would you want it any other way? You're in for something weird, wild and ugly but in this embrace of ugliness, you find an honesty that's actually quite beautiful.

— Garrett Cook, editor

A LETTER FROM THE AUTHOR

Dearest reader I feel that this book is a Zombie of sorts. That even after it's death, after I murdered it myself, I cannot stop thinking about it. It seems to wander about my mind, stinking up the place. Well no more. Consider this edition me setting it free of my brain and hopefully giving it the attention is deserves.

- Leigham Shardlow

CHAPTER 1

The wind buffeted the almost perfect skin of the immaculate Adonis. The huge g-forces from the fall did not affect his taut bronzed naked flesh at all; not one ripple or cropped hair moved out of place. He was whooping with absolute joy at the sensation of diving headfirst to the ground. The grey city below him was in miniature but kept growing in size with every second of his enforced free fall.

He opened his arms and legs as like a star with minimal effort, slowing slightly, his enormous cock and balls flapped back and forth from the buffeting wind, slapping his inner thighs loudly.

He heard beautiful, graceful, perfect laughter behind him getting ever closer. Often she streamed right past him, curvaceous and thin in all the right places for him, an icon of perfection. Her long blonde hair seemed alive in the colossal updraft of their fall, glistening in the bright sun, gorgeous, sexy snakes full of life and vigour.

She fell through a bright white cloud disappearing for

a second. The Adonis felt sadness for the first time in his life, seeing her disappear so suddenly it was akin to the grief of thousand loved one's dying. A second later he entered the cloud and almost instantaneously exploded out the other side drenched in cold sky water, which quickly froze on his skin and flaked off into the ether like diamond dust, sparkling in the bright sun.

He saw her face for the first time and his cock became as hard as steel and his balls crunched against himself tight and full. She had managed to turn up to face him in the few seconds he had taken his eyes off hers. She smiled elegantly and beckoned him closer with her finger. The Adonis did as he did before, making himself dart like with his arms by his side and legs behind him so that streamed through the sky so much faster.

The closer she got, the more intense his erection seemed, almost feeling like he would explode if he couldn't touch her. He stretched out his muscled arm trying to touch her similarly outstretched hand.

Two inches, one inch, he was so close, a millennium of seconds passed, until his hand managed to grasp hers. He ejaculated instantly, as they hit the top of the dirty concrete building's angled roof. They bounced off, limbs broken and twisted into almost impossible angles, leaving smears of red gore on the edge of the building.

Blood spurted and floated with them as they barrelled through the air. For less than a heartbeat they locked eyes once more, sharing ultimate passion in their gaze, before smashing head first into the road beneath them at fifty three meters per second, exploding like a grenade into jelly and bone fragments.

The bone fragments shot out in all directions, a carnage nail bomb made of people, penetrating the soft flesh of a family out for a Saturday stroll. They were covered in dark purple birthmarks and boils. A thigh bone impaled the smallest child through the skull, killing her instantly. The rest of the family received minor cuts but inner scars so deep that they were lost to madness in the coming days.

They began screaming at their daughter's corpse, the rest of the street joining them. When they stopped looking at the grisly scene in the middle of the road and looked upwards the sky was blocked out by billions more falling people hurtling towards them. The city joined in the cry of terror as well-groomed chaos began to fall onto the last ugly city in the world.

———

F at Janet, Obese Janet to her friends, mercilessly beat the dirty man again with her walking stick. She swung it over her head in huge circular arcs, the folds under her arms flapping like wings with each connecting swing, with a resulting thud of willow against bone. The homeless man clung onto the plastic bag full of brightly coloured tubes, as did Janet with one arm and her considerable strength.

"Back off fuck-o, these are my biscuits! Go buy your gosh darn own," grunted Fat Janet with vigour and spite enforced into every syllable.

She put more force into her hits and cracked him on his nose, which crumpled like tissue paper under the force but didn't bleed. He let go of the bag and stumbled backwards a few steps, holding his misshapen prosthesis in one hand.

"Oi! You's got a fake plastic nose! We don't like plastic people in this city. Shun him!" she screamed full of hate.

The small crowd of amputees that had gathered to watch the homeless bashing began jeering and screeching "Hit him!" repeatedly as a form of chant.

"OI Nosey, Fakey Nosey," shouted a young boy with missing ears, just holes in the side of his head, whilst spitting on the man's dirty but fashionable shoes. The homeless man grabbed his nose with both hands trying to reform it back into shape, he then pushed his way through the crowd, crying and running as fast as his well-toned legs would carry him. His sandals smacking the dirty tarmac in a regular rhythm and poise as if he had been professionally taught how to walk. He finally crunched his nose back into its perfect shape, smooth skinned, clear of blackheads and marks, yet oddly roman in shape. It complimented his symmetrical face perfectly. The nose had been costly to make and even more expensive to have fitted, hours of surgery and sacrifice only to be insulted for it. The shame of it all.

Fat Janet watched him leave through angry, small eyes and then turned to the crowd swinging the walking stick over her head in huge arcing circles again, letting it whistle silently through the air.

"You lot can fuck off as well!" She screamed putting her foot on the accelerator of her electric scooter and driving, still swinging the walking stick, into the crowd which parted rather sharpish for a group of disabled people with only half the legs they were born with.

―――――

T he homeless man sat down on his cardboard box, lamenting his empty stomach. Reaching underneath him he rooted through the contents of his box, pulling out a faded and dirty copy of Exquisite Skin. His own not much younger visage adorned the cover, in full archbishop regalia complete with the traditional tight black hot pants, velvet robes and a Pontiff hat made of delicate gold leaf. He was beautiful beyond compare. The faded blue caption underneath read "New Cardinal appointed by Flesh Pope." He shook the magazine to bits with rage, his face twisted into a snarl of anger at that fat woman.

"That fat ugly selfish bitch. I hate her and all the horrible, ungrateful and ugly people. Most of all, I hate this city full of ugly sin!" he screamed into the only piece of magazine he had managed to keep a hold of, his own solemn and pious face smiling coyly back at him.

He reached into his jacket pocket and pulled out a crumpled up piece of newspaper. It was an advert designed to attract tourists. Big bold type and simple language screamed at him to throw it away.

"COME TO DISFIGURE-BURG! The last ugly city on the PLANET!! All freaks welcome, come for the unbelievable property prices, and stay for the community!!"

He blew his nose noisily on it after reading and threw it over his shoulder.

The alley he was in was his own. No one would come near him and his flawless face and immaculately sculpted beard, they wouldn't dare be seen with the likes of him. He was wrong and unnatural in this place. They spat at him and cursed his being like he was leper, which was ironic because this place was full of actual lepers.

"Dammit," he said to himself whilst frantically tapping the side of his head with his hand, a habit he had acquired since being exiled here.

"I was the best plastic surgeon ever. I could have turned this whole city into a fucking paradise." He stood up and gestured grandly to the road in the front of him pontificating with the picture of his face grandly.

"FUCK YOU, DISFIGURED TURD! You don't know what you're missing! My works have been looked upon and adored by those incapable of love! I am change!" He tore off his ragged coat and unveiled his clean and immaculate plastic robes, the height of priestly fashion before he had to leave the rest of his old world.

A disgusting family strolled past, their purple pocked skin reflecting the bright sun in a sickly way, they were all smiling happily. The homeless man stared at them with scorn and gobbed on the dirty concrete floor of the alley. "Ugly, ugly, ugly," he muttered to himself.

There was a loud wet crunch and one of the family let out their last breaths as they were skewered with bone shrapnel from above. The homeless man was shielded from most the projectiles but a large piece embedded itself in his bicep.

He yelled out in pain and wrenched it out in an arc of blood. He gazed at the yellow bone, looking it over and found it was shaped like a thin half-moon. To him it was a scalpel, thin, delicate and covered in blood. As it should be.

"It's a sign. A wonderful sign. I must make them all beautiful. So perfect like me." He cried tears of joy as he tore open his ceremonial robes, revealing that underneath he wore stained and dirty surgical scrubs, stained with a thousand operations to bring those into the fold of beauty. "Cardinal Slice will take his patients now, I will remake these things into something divine," he said conceding the fact that his surgical scrubs would be stained once more with a thousand more saved souls.

———

It was silent at the old church on Green Hill. It had been left abandoned for decades but its iron spires and grand stained glass windows had stood the test of time and, the many vandals, as the faded but graphically rude graffiti showed.

Inside, a woman stood naked amongst the decimated pews. She danced sultry at the pulpit, her loose old skin hanging like an empty condom off a toilet seat. Waving her hand she let drops of her blood fall from her self cut hand, splashing into the full cauldron. The iron pot swirled, smoked and sparkled with black magic, essence of perfume and sparkle unicorn glitter, which she had gotten from the Love Crafts store on the way up to the church.

Then she let out the high, shrill laugh that she thought most witches must sound like. It was her first time doing proper magic, all her friends would be so jealous of how cool she could still be at her age, seventy four years young.

It was also her last magic spell as herself, before she could utter any incantation the skylight above her broke and twenty sculpted gods and goddesses fell on her instantly crushing her to death, spilling the cauldrons essence and fluids, which leaked out from underneath the pile of bodies. The concoction was stained red, with the glitter still sparkling in the early morning light that streamed through the stained glass windows.

CHAPTER 2

J anet had taken shelter inside the Stuck Pig Eatery. She didn't like to come here at all but their all you can eat trough special helped her when the money got thin, which it often did. She would often pretend to be eating but would scoop the best bits of pizza and fried chicken into her bra and underpants to store in her chest freezer when she got home.

There were no windows in here. Patrons of the Stuck Pig liked their privacy when they ate, or to be more accurate gorged, on the fastest of foods. Although implicitly encouraged by the local government, tourism to their city was hated by those that had to live there. Especially Fat Janet. Janet wouldn't leave her apartment for days at a time, just to avoid having her photo taken.

The bodies outside fell like rain in a thunderstorm, each crunch and splat joined by a hundred more as they hit the fifty story high, stainless steel shell of the restaurant's mascot, Crackling, a piglet posed halfway into the

Charleston. It wore a solid steel bowler hat, which was ever too small for its head. Heavy thuds echoed through Cracklin and the building, making Janet's bones ache with sympathy at every impact.

The owner, a legless man who rode around in a wheeled wooden cart, sat comforting a bald overweight woman, who lay on the floor in his lap. Each sob made ripples vibrate through the woman's waterlogged body. The rest of the patrons were either stood or sat near the huge silver trough that snaked around the edge of the room. The centre was a closed off island containing the kitchen and, from what Janet had been told, a ladder to the top of Cracklin's Bowler hat.

There was at least ten other people in here with them, most of them being regular patrons that had been gorging on the Saturday spaghetti special before the people had begun falling. Janet knew it wasn't uncommon for people to spend days in here only to be ejected when they fell unconscious through lack of sleep. She was sort of proud that they had the freedom to do that to themselves, it was their lives and she didn't judge them for what they did to themselves, only what they did to other people who got in their way of the trough. She'd seen some horrible acts of violence in the name of cheap fried chicken.

"Are we safe in here?" asked a small child wearing just a pair of swimming shorts. Its hairless body was covered in red, gaping, raw sores. Janet couldn't bear to look past its androgynous, fearful and tearful eyes. She could barely contain her own nerves, her hands shaking slightly with terror.

The owner cleared his throat and smiled slightly. "Ole Cracklin should...errm ...deflect any of them from hitting the roof. Main... errm ...problems... not them outside, though, it's the contents of the errm kitchen and freezer, or should that be the errm lack of contents of the errm kitchen. We've not had our order since errm, yes, yesterday."

The large woman in his lap looked up and around at everyone with red swollen eyes.

"Get rid of the stranger," she said matter-of-factly through chipped and yellow teeth in a voice like she was speaking through cloth. Janet noticed she was holding a dirty blonde coloured wig in her chubby mitts and was pointing at her with it.

Most of the patrons looked at Janet with guilty looks, as if they knew what was coming.

"Hey, I eat here all the time. I'm Fat Janet remember guys?" she blurted out in the nicest tone of voice she could muster. Which was alien to Janet even when she spoke to her cat, Puddin Pop.

"I don't know you!" screamed a man whose saggy folds of flesh burst from under his bright pink logo emblazoned t shirt. She had seen this man in here before and although having seen his stomach more times than she would have wanted, never had she seen hide nor hare of a belly button. It disturbed her to think of it.

"You best leave before they errm, yes, eat you!" said the owner from the floor.

"Eat me? That's mad. There's still food in the kitchen you said. That's what you said!" said Janet, her anxiety starting to creep into her voice, a slight quiver to match her shaking hands.

"Well, yeah, but they'll be free to munch on the carpet themselves. I'm still going to charge people for the main trough meal. Man's got to make a living even when the world ends. You, though, you don't have any money."

"Hey, man, I'm not eating carpet!" Shouted Logo Man, sweeping his hand through his long, greasy black hair.

"Baby, I get to eat for free though?" the bald woman began rubbing the owner's crotch, with her massive hands. Tough she was rubbing too hard for it to be pleasurable he had a small erection, Fat Janet noticed it and threw up a bit in her throat.

"If you get rid of her and errm maybe scratch my back later, yes you can eat for free," he replied before whispering something Janet didn't catch into her ear for a few seconds. The woman giggled in response.

"I've been in here for barely five minutes. Look, I'll leave once this whole thing stops, honest." Fat Janet was starting to cry.

The large waterlogged woman stood up and took a few tentative steps forwards, her dress strangely flattering against the bulbous-ness of her limbs, her wig dropped to the floor forgotten. She reached over the handlebars and turned the key on Janet's scooter before half pushing her towards the door. Janet put her feet on the floor as a form of brake. The scooter was old and the brakes only worked when it was already in motion.

"Come on, help me, you fat load of bastards!" the waterlogged woman screamed at the rest of the patrons.

They all rushed forwards. The owner wheeled himself towards the door and held it open, instantly becoming coated in dollops of gore as he did so. The thunder of the people hail from outside covered up the screams of Fat Janet's protests and the grunts of the other patrons trying to push the scooter and Fat Janet out the door.

The scooter rocked back and forth as Janet resisted and with a few shakes she was tipped out. She cried out in pain, landing awkwardly on her leg. The patrons didn't give her time to catch her breath and before she knew it, Fat Janet had been literally rolled out of the door into the street.

Even above the noise of the people falling from the sky, Fat Janet heard the door slam behind her.

"You utter selfish cunts!" she screamed back at the door, trying her best to get up. It was slow going but she had to move fast, something would hit her any moment. Something did.

A figure barrelled into the side of her, knocking them both clear of a rather over muscled woman who hit the floor where they she had just been standing, she had been deflected off the giant form of Cracklin and travelled at a slight angle, slowing down somewhat. It hit the floor and skidded several feet past them, eventually slamming into the side of a car leaving a trail of blood and entrails behind her.

The figure that had slammed into Janet got itself up quickly and helped Janet to her feet. The man was generally average in appearance, clean shaven, an extra thumb and finger hung awkwardly from his cheek but fairly non-descript in this city thought Janet.

"Can you run?" he asked, patting down his brown jacket. Janet looked across the street most of the buildings had been barred shut quite quickly, she could see the people hiding far in the back or piling things up against the windows.

"Yes but where?" she asked.

"The alley, quick!"

He grabbed her hand quite firmly and they half jogged to the side of the Stuck Pig, its neon sign had been smashed and only read "Eat." Janet barely registered that, as they rushed around the corner and over some bags filled with empty refill cups.

There was a crash behind them as a body exploded where they had just been standing not a few seconds before. She looked up at the twenty storey high imposing figure of Cracklin. It was dented and covered in bloodstains but still smiled with a greedy, gleeful mouth full of metal strips, which Fat Janet assumed to be bacon. She watched in awe as they reached the end of the first alleyway, seeing a rather buxom brunette slamming into the top of Cracklin's bowler hat, exploding into a shower of human detritus. Blood showered down onto the bags behind her. The short pitter-patter made her throw up a little bit in her mouth. Fat Janet looked away and concentrated on the alley in front of them. They came bursting out of the alley into a small cul-de-sac used for the local bus station. The entrance to which was wide open and inviting.

"In the bus station, hurry," the man yelled, letting go of her hand. Fat Janet could feel her lungs on fire and her legs turning to jelly.

The bus station entrance wasn't far. Janet took a few steps forward but stopped when the body of a thin long-haired man, with just the best six-pack, slammed into the pavement in front of her peppering her with bone and coating her with chunks of intestines.

She fell backwards in stinging pain, landing on her backside. Janet's exposed forearms had started bleeding from the bone fragments impacting on them. She couldn't tell what was her blood and what wasn't but at this point but she knew the pain and stinging meant it was at least a little of hers.

As her saviour had reached the entrance, he had stopped dead in his tracks. He took two steps backwards with his hands held up. Janet could tell something was horribly wrong. There was a gunshot and the man half swerved, half ran back towards her, yelling something that she couldn't hear over the roaring of her heart pounding in her chest and a second gunshot.

She scrambled to her feet as he reached her. Grabbing her arm above the elbow, this time he ran her the other way towards the underpass that lead into the cul-de-sac. Janet forced her huge legs to scramble madly after his, he was much faster than her and she was afraid that if she didn't keep up she would fall again or that his hand would slip off because of the blood that coated them both.

They reached the underpass, running all the way down the incline in order to be fully safe from any detritus from the bodies. Janet pulled the man into a hug but quickly pushed him away in embarrassment.

"Sorry, just, oh my chest is on fire and all of this it's, it's too much," she panted out in small gasps.

"Just sit down and breathe, we'll make it through this somehow, I promise," he replied.

She sat down on the curb and looked up at him, the orange lights of the underpass didn't make him look any less normal, though he looked slightly more handsome to her but she dismissed the thought as probably a trick of the bright lights.

"I'm Isaac," he said sitting down next to her with a thud.

"Fat Janet," she replied still panting.

"Have you got any smokes, Janet?"

"Not at all, those things will definitely kill you."

He smiled like it was the first time. Fat Janet just stared at her orthopaedic shoes and tried to avoid eye contact. Not even her own parents had been this nice to her.

CHAPTER 3

"**J**ohnson, that's it, isn't it?"

"Yes, Cardinal?" Victor Johnson was about three foot tall wet through, although he was dry now so probably about two foot five. He stood at attention in his janitor overalls leaning on a rather large antiquated shotgun.

Cardinal Slice placed his perfectly manicured hand gently on Johnson's shoulder, bending over to do so.

"Nobody in or out of our temporary temple, Johnson. I know you know of the word of the flesh. Others need to be educated in the correct sacrifices required for inner peace and fulfilment. To stop this madness, for that, I need privacy away from fearful sheep. At least for the time being."

Cardinal Slice pulled him back from the door slightly as a body collided with the road in front of the bus station. Johnson was grateful his overalls had been saved from the mess.

"Thank you, your worship. I, I mean we, we here are

all grateful for you leading us out of this, this hell, to safety. My gun and heart are yours to use as you wish." "We'll need more than a gun to tackle the horror that the fall from the heavens presents. Your trust in me will be enough for now but we have so much to accomplish in such a short time. Johnson, I believe in you and our exodus will be guided by your hands. Keep them steady."

Slice wandered back into the station, knowing that Johnson would keep his post. Whether he failed to protect them would serve as another matter to handle later. These, lost souls, would need a firm guiding hand and he would have to be quick to mould them into the forms their souls longed for.

There was a racket from out behind the building with a giant pig on it. Johnson disliked that place, no windows meant he couldn't see inside. They could be doing anything in there, disgusting, and horrible things.

Johnson watched the woman being half dragged by the man out of the alley before they separated and she fell on her lard-filled knees. He stilled himself by gripping the shotgun harder.

"Nobody in," he repeated to himself. It hadn't been a minute but the command guided his thoughts and actions as if by some unseen, yet holy, force. He raised the gun upward, aiming towards the man's face as he ran closer. The thumb and finger protruding from the man's face looked off somehow, but Johnson had a job to do, he had no time to think of things like that.

"Fuck off!" he screamed over the noise of the people hitting the tarmac of the cul-de-sac. The man didn't seem to hear him at all, continuing to run full pelt towards him.

Johnson wasn't a cruel man, or quick to anger but he hated to be ignored more than anything that this horrible world had thrown at him.

"I said back off man! This isn't a joke. No one gets the, fuck, in here!"

The man stopped and put his hands up in protest. He was shouting something but that feeling of being willed to action flowed through Johnson again, his adrenaline pushed his hearing out and all he could concentrate on was the trigger tensing under his finger. He raised the shotgun high above this desperate stranger and fired. Finally getting the hint, the man ran off in the other direction back towards the now kneeling fat bitch, only stopping to help up the woman as they ran off to the underpass at the far end.

"Can't imagine they'll be much more out in this, utter, hell," he said to himself, repeating the Cardinals choice of language before letting the gun come to rest on the ground.

"At least no one aimless running around like those idiots," he muttered under his breath knowing he meant they would either best get to hiding or be dead very soon.

———

Cardinal Slice had gathered the rest of his, beauties-to-be in the main foyer of the station. Some lay on the cheap plastic moulded chairs resting or recovering from superficial wounds caused by the falling people.

The rest, about thirty of them, had stood around him in a semi-circle. He didn't want to look on their missing limbs, strange birth defects or discoloured skin. They reminded him of the work that must be done and the pain these misguided creatures would endure. He felt solace and meaning in his grief at their and his own sacrifice that was come but he must redeem himself here, in the worst kind of horror that had befallen this city.

"People, good people, honest people. I am here to serve you in these troubling and terrifying times." he intended to begin a larger speech but was quickly interrupted by a greasy teenager with grey pallid skin and boils the size of tennis balls clumped around his neck skin.

"Now wait just a minute, do you know what's happening? Why it's happening?" said Boily-O. Slice had begun naming people by their afflictions and physical features in his head until he had some better reason to remember them, servitude or sacrifice would be enough, probably.

"Yeah, who are you? With those fancy clothes and your nice hair. You look like them tourists. Like a statue." this came from what he assumed to be a woman.

Her facial features were enlarged to an uncomfortable degree by elephantiasis but her hair was cropped short and dyed lime green. He didn't like her at all.

"Are we going to die?" came another rather deep voice from the back.

"Where's my family?" A gruff older one he couldn't tell the sex of.

"How are we going to survive?" Asked a mature man.

"Do we have enough food?"

"When will this stop?"

"I'm scared."

"I'm angry." "Please help us."

They all began shouting over one another, a panicked moan of utter confusion and terror. Slice's heart raced and he raised his arms and intended to shout for some semblance of order.

The small skylight above him broke and shards of bones, glass and blood rained down onto him. Yet they missed Slice entirely. Everything around the Cardinal, including the future beauties stood near him, had been splattered in the fresh gore, but not the Cardinal, he was spotless.

They all stared in silence, as if his raised arms called the miracle into birth.

"See!" Slice pontificated loudly, quickly recognising his opportunity.

"See the works of myself. Cardinal of the skin, changer of flesh and beholder of beauty. I am untouched because I have scoured myself of the uncleanliness of outside and embraced my soul's true form through advanced surgery techniques."

They all moved forward slowly and began to touch Slices face all at once, coating him in the blood and, to his displeasure, offal of the recent splattered bodies. Anointing him as their saviour.

"Yes, feel what you can be for you. I can give you protection and so much more. Through change, through actualizing the inner truth, through me and my hands, through your own determination, through your pain, can we rise and conquer anything this nightmare from the sky will literally throw at us. I believe in you my wonderful beauties. We can not only survive this we can stop it. It's the truth, with my knife, your willing skin and faith that the flesh will be better than anything you can imagine."

He beckoned them backwards with slow waves of his hands.

"Sit my beauties, take some time to reflect on the disingenuous drabs your souls inhabit that you must shake off. For the outside will change to fit the inside. Casting off the vestments of the past will be more difficult that you could ever imagine and I am here to guide you through this. Lean on me and you can be free of yourselves."

———

Blood was flowing into the grate at the lowest point of the underpass. The now dull orange lights made it seem inky black, like iron rich oil. Fat Janet stared at it, while Isaac wandered near the exit opposite to the one they came in by. They had been down here a good hour and the falling bodies had only increased in rate. Several times Isaac had wandered up that way to check on the situation and each time he came back he had worse and worse news.

He slowly walked backed down shaking his head sadly. "Still no slowing down?" she asked.

"Yeah it's only getting worse. I imagine they'll begin to pile up soon. Do you think they're dead before they hit the ground?"

"I heard that falling at that speed can give you a heart attack," Janet replied.

"I don't know. I mean they don't make a lot of noise besides you know, the crunch," He winced when he said the word "crunch."

"What time is it do you think it is?" asked Fat Janet "Got to be about two in the afternoon. The suns still high and I'm sure I heard a church's bell ringing earlier. Then again, it could just be them bouncing off that giant, grotesque metal pig."

"I'm missing my stories on the boob tube," lamented Janet

"I can tell you a story if you want?" offered Isaac as he sat next to her. Janet shuffled away from him. Being near anyone that close when they were not eating made her so uncomfortable.

"I would like that. Tell me about yourself Isaac, I've never seen you around before. Not that I get out much."

"Okay. I used to be married. I had the biggest most beautiful farm house and my job was complicated but I got to help people. Or at least I thought I was helping people."

"Tell me about your wife."

"Oh, husband."

"I'm sorry, I just assumed that..." She trailed off in embarrassment.

"It's fine, honestly. We weren't together for very long, he errm well. I don't look it but I'm almost sixty. I married for love and loneliness. I was very lucky to marry someone wonderful."

Janet looked at him and couldn't see a single grey hair

or wrinkle. He must have had something done. She didn't blame him for it but it wasn't her way. Those religious nutters always made you go through so much guilt before they would touch you. It was too much for her to lie to herself like that. Fat Janet she was to herself so she would stay that way. He continued on with his story oblivious to her day dreaming.

"I met him whilst he was in his teens, he was so thin and his nose like a little strawberry. Stick-like but he was passionate about poetry, truth and love. He would stroke my hair and would read to me until I fell asleep," Isaac started crying, Janet put her hand on his shoulder.

"I'm ok I want to talk about him. It just hurts so much, you know?" he continued.

Janet nodded, agreeing but not knowing herself. "We got married in June, it was cold and raining. I wanted sun, a summer wedding and it fucking rained. We were so drunk and happy though. At least I was happy. I had signed myself to him. We let each other be in charge of our flesh. It seemed right, that it would make him happy. It did for a while until well, you know he die.....died...." he trailed off, softly sobbing to himself.

Janet reached over and held his hand as he began to cry harder.

"You don't have to go on if you don't want to," said Janet.

"No it's fine. We used to go boating on the river in our home town in the summer, let nature baptize us he would say. One summer he drove us out to the boathouse where our boat was moored. I should have known something was wrong, he never drove. We pulled off at the wrong turn and went thirty miles in the wrong direction. I didn't want to correct him, he hated that. Used to give me the silent treatment, then he'd call me directionless before everything went back to normal."

For the first time, the thumping in the background wasn't full force in Janet's mind, she had forgotten its presence.

"Thirty miles in the wrong direction, I should have known. It was so easy to see that something would go wrong. We stopped outside a church for directions and the priests came running out and dragged me from then car. They saved me, but the other car just, smashed into, oh god I can see his face Janet."

"Did he die?"

"I'm sorry, I can't go on."

Janet let go of his hand, the story didn't make much sense in her head. The church of the skin would not have tolerated that finger and thumb on his face. They would have let the car hit him. Why was he here? Isaac was at least hiding something and at most lying to her. For the first time since meeting him Fat Janet was afraid of Isaac, she couldn't trust him.

Isaac wiped the tears from his eyes on the back of his shirt sleeve.

"Tell me a story Janet? Did you ever love anyone?"

"No. It's just been me, my cat, the boob tube and the fridge." She lied, Janet loved herself dearly.

"Oh. Well I'm sure you'll have a story to tell after today, it's fucking crazy out there."

CHAPTER 4

J ohnson would be the voice of the new way, the old way, the right way. He has been blessed with a new face, carved out of glass and the moulded sacred meat from the sky. It was swollen and bruised but once it had healed the Cardinal had told him that he wouldn't need to speak his divine message it would beam from his smile and his features would dance in the converts minds forever.

Johnson, asked for a script anyway, at least twenty percent of the city was blind in some way.

"You should be able to feel beauty with the touch as well as with the eye," the Cardinal had preached at his fourth sermon that first day after he had shown his power to avoid those that fell from the sky.

He had guided them safely through the side streets entering homes and businesses spreading the word. Then, that night, his worship would forgo sleep and spend all night bestowing his follows with new faces and bodies with nothing more than the tools that were bestowed upon him from the sky and the sacred glass from the miracle.

Johnson stepped out in the morning drizzle making his way from the prosthetics shop using his shotgun to stop himself slipping on the rushing rivers of thick blood. The restaurant with the giant metal pig on the roof would be his first test at convergence. Others had left before him and had been hit by those that fell, or slipped on some intestines and had been carried away with the rushing blood tide not to be seen by him again. It was a test of his will and his faith. He strolled carefully out into the tide. A body crashed to his right, spraying with gunk from the river. Wiping it from his eyes, he ran, plodding onwards and leading with the butt of his shotgun, which slipped more than once on some unseen organ, yet he kept his footing.

He saw an almost complete leg float past, Johnson tried to use his shotgun to drag it closer but it was drawn away too fast. Shaking his head he trudged on forwards, one step at a time but with the speed of fear in his tiny feet.

He made it to the door of the restaurant and tried to wrench it open. It shook in its frame and resisted his pull. The door had been barricaded from the inside. Johnson wouldn't be denied, this was another test of his will. He moved around the side of the building to find another way in.

The entire side alley was piled high with piles of bone and meat, yet on top was an almost complete body sans head, cushioned by its brothers and sisters from the fall. Enough to survive mostly intact but obviously not alive. He was crying at the sight of its broken body for the wonders that the Cardinal could bestow on his flock could never compare to the ultimate sight of this wondrous, perfectly proportioned corpse.

He would have to take it to show the others, this was why he couldn't get into the restaurant; he was guided to this holy site, to see something more sacred than the works of Cardinal Slice.

———

J anet hadn't slept, the constant pounding and cracking of bone was replaced with a wet smack of meat on meat. She pretended the sound was balls of mud being thrown into a pond, anything to get her mind off the reality of what was actually happening.

Isaac wasn't asleep either, he was watching them fall from a close enough perspective without getting splashed. Janet watched him pace back and forth, the lights of the underpass illuminating him too well, so he looked like a demon had crept into his skin and took a shit.

"Has it slowed down?" she asked, getting up from her sitting position.

"Getting worse, you can't see the street anymore."

"I'm hungry, tired and scared, Isaac. What is going on?"

"I know about as much as you do but I know we'll need to move soon, we're lower than them."

Janet hadn't really noticed but blood had begun to gather in a large puddle. The drainage grate in the middle of the underpass had backed up and refused any more gore.

"Do you think it'll flood completely?" she asked. "Probably but I'm more worried about that nutter with gun from earlier. I saw him and a group of, err people just leave the bus station not long ago."

"In this?" she asked, ignoring the pause in the middle of his sentence. Some people didn't like the way she looked, a conversation without a silence instead of an insult was a nice one, or at least that's what the cat poster on her wall said.

"Yeah, scary, right? Fear makes people do crazy things but a group of people just walking out there is just suicide. Could be a bunch of fleshites trying to save other people, I suppose."

"I've never met a cult before."

Isaac looked at her quizzically.

"What?"

"We need to move," he said, changing the conversation.

"What now? You just said it's suicidal to go walking in this and then you suggest it. I'm terrified and I want to go home but I'm not that desperate to die, Isaac."

"It's getting faster, I've been keeping count and the longer we stay here, the worse it'll get."

"Ok, fine. Beats drowning I guess," she said, resigning herself to death. Janet was exhausted and wanted out of everything.

Fat Janet hobbled over to Isaac. Her legs had gone slightly numb from sitting on the floor for so long.

"Can I hold your hand though?" she asked.

He grasped it firmly and led her up the short ramp to the exit of the underpass and they looked out. Everything that wasn't illuminated by the yellow street lamps was slick and black in the night. Abandoned cars, crumpled and mangled by the impacts lay crisscrossed hastily across the roads.

"I'm ready," said Isaac.

Janet took a breath and pulled Isaac through the cars and into the nearest doorway of a plain brick accommodation houses within a few seconds. Not one body had fallen near them or hit the cars next to them.

"A guardian," whispered Isaac.

Then a body slammed into one of the cars, impacting on the windscreen making glass and guts fly in all directions hitting the nearby cars and setting off a loud, piercing alarm on one of them.

Janet tried the door and it opened easily. They rushed inside slamming it behind them. They were safer in here, hiding out the horror that was out in the streets. They looked around the poorly lit lobby with green tiled everything. Without speaking they climbed up the stairs making for a high room to hide.

"We should lock the door," said Janet.

"Probably but what if someone else like us wants to use it, I couldn't have that on my conscious." He smiled. They passed a window and Janet caught her reflection for the first time in what seemed like years. Dried blood caked her skin, the brown rough texture of it did nothing to hide the how tired and drained she was. No tear streaks though, she hadn't cried which gave her some hope.

Every door they passed was locked and the screams of the tenants to leave them alone quickly stopped them from trying. Janet couldn't carry on. Each step made her wheeze harder and her legs to ache more. They stopped on the third floor there, too horrified to sleep, too tired to stay awake, they sat on the floor. Holding each other's hands tightly Janet and Isaac waited in silence for the end of the world.

———

It had taken Slice a good few hours to reach the one hundredth floor, the lifts were not working, but the view was majestic. Through the plain glass windows he saw the huge block towers, pillars of undeserved growth and prosperity laid out beneath him and the blurs kept falling. Its streets were hard to make out now as the bodies had piled up at an impossible two stories high. They filled the streets to the brim and were pressing against the sides of the buildings, breaking the glass windows of some buildings and pouring in like water into a ruptured submarine.

He turned his back on the view and faced old Margaret who was bound to a wheelchair. A set of surgical tools placed on a bedside table next to her shone even in the dull grey sunlight.

She was blind since birth; she had barely noticed when maggots had eaten the eyes out of her skull at aged twenty. Her skin was taut and a thin yellow, the maggots had eaten some of that as well and her nose was just two gaping holes that shone into the echoes of her skull.

"Before this Cardinal, I was a teacher of ethics at the university. I tried to instil the values of others happiness over your own. I shouldn't be here, I should be out spreading your word like the others," she said, her voice like cracked silk.

"Shhh. Those thoughts are ghosts of your past self. We're here to change everyone and when they see you, a perfect visage of light and the ultimate beauty. You'll be spreading more joy than you could ever imagine."

"I'm so happy your grace."

"Child take a deep breath, the pain of transformation will begin."

He took up his scalpel and began to delicately slice the right side of her face. The blade tucked gently under skin and a tear drop of blood flowed before it. He continued until she had a smooth red circle around her face, separating her skin from the muscles beneath. Slice placed the bloody scalpel down and picked up a section of piano wire tied between two wooden handles. "Oh the token we have been blessed with, the rights so given freely to mould we are forever thankful. Amen," he whispered to his tool.

He placed the wire underneath the top lip of Margaret's still bleeding face cut. He quickly moved the wire side to side, wrenching chunks of her skin and flesh off in long strips that flew to ground around them. Margaret began screaming and thrashing when he got to her nose hole. Long strips of blood, salty tears and mucus from her nose began to drip off in long slimy tendrils from her still clean chin.

"Let me finish, woman!" he bellowed before

punching her in the head. The force of the hit cracked her frail skull and she lopped forward silent.

Cardinal Slice threw the piano wire on the table with a crash in frustration.

"Unworthy bitch!"

He walked behind the wheelchair and pushed it with as much force as he could muster, letting it fly through the window, smashing into pieces before Margaret fell ninety eight stories and with a soft plop landed on the mounds of the dead.

Slice walked to the lifts behind him and pressed the open button. As the doors slid apart from each other, he knelt next to the shrine inside. The body of the woman Johnson had brought back lay in side, cleaned and covered with many candles. He lit one of them and pressed the lobby button. As he exited knowing his followers would see his sign and another potential apostle would ride up to be transformed and deemed worthy by himself.

When he had seen the body that Johnson had brought back Slice knew he had to surpass it. He had contemplated for a few hours not knowing how to do it. Then he had vision of supreme, divine beauty, a beauty he could create.

As an eight foot tall man with a square head stepped out of the elevator. Slice smiled to himself, his work was far from over.

———

"I won't fit," Janet argued.

"We don't have much of choice we have to make it to higher ground, before we're buried and trapped in here," said Isaac.

They were on the top floor of the small apartment building, the midday sun streaking through the last window not blocked with broken body parts.

"Fine but I go first so you can push me out."

"Deal."

Janet pushed the small window up and pushed her right arm and head out the window. Using her legs she pushed forwards and became stuck fast.

"I fucking told you," she screamed back at him whilst desperately trying not touch the gore inches from her hand.

She heard Isaac take a few steps back before he began running. Janet felt the force of his charge and grunting, she moved forward a few inches. Isaac did this three more times until Janet was able to pull her other arm out of the window.

"Let me do the rest, Isaac."

She heard him running forwards. "Isaac stop!"

Isaac slammed into her and Janet was launched out of the window like a cork. She somersaulted head over arse and landed on the battered corpse of what looked like a blonde woman with massive boobs.

"Isaac, you prick."

Then the pile began to tremble, she felt it shift downwards and before Janet could cry out the piles of mottled body parts swallowed her whole. Isaac stared transfixed and dumbfounded from the window as Janet disappeared underneath the bloody mass of meat and bone.

He leapt through the window and began digging with his bare hands, throwing the chunks of raw flesh, organs and hair over his shoulder. He kept going for a full hour until he collapsed from exhaustion.

As he lay on his back, his clothes soaking through with the blood and bile that pooled here and there. Isaac looked upwards noticing that for the first time the bodies had stopped falling from the sky.

———

Janet's mouth filled with the thick black soup as the tide of collapsing bodies rushed past her. The weight of the blood and bodies pushed her downwards and the open chasm beneath her seemed never-ending. Engulfing her like an unseen blanket of gore, Janet could do nothing but roll and violently grasp at anything solid. She managed to grasp something metallic and cold.

"A lamppost," she thought but her grip wasn't strong enough and she was once again barrelled along, this time sideways. Her lungs screaming and her stomach trying to vomit against the mouth full of blood and bile that wasn't her own.

After what seemed like an age Fat Janet was flushed out onto a flat surface, free of the still moving wave of flesh. She rolled a few feet and slowed to halt. She choked and spit all the vile mess into a heap, before her stomach finally voided itself onto the mess.

Janet breathed heavily, coughing after each breath before slowly getting to her feet.

She was in a virtually pitch black corridor. Inset into walls at irregular points she saw the dim lights of flashlights that illuminated sections of the opposite wall. Janet limped to the nearest one and saw that the meat had been scraped away. Small canals in the green flesh and black organs had been carved into the walls. Huge holes dotted here and there denoted the removal of bones.

Janet shuddered when she noticed that the channels were in groups of four, as if done by bare hands, manic and purposeful. A torn off fingernail stuck fast into the meat proved this, Janet recoiled at it stepping away from her inspection. She walked to the opposite wall and took out the flashlight that had been crudely rested into one the bone holes.

Shining the dim light of the low battery torch around Janet saw that the whole tunnel had been dug the same. Looking behind her Janet saw the quicksand of guts and muscle that she fell through had halted and blocked the tunnel. Slowly using the flashlight to illuminate the dugout floor. Janet walked the only way forward, terrified of where it would lead.

CHAPTER 5

I saac walked through the echoes of civilization, meandering through the empty spaces between the tallest buildings on tarmac built from the rotting dead. Each step was a gamble as to whether it was uneven, marshy, or like sickly quicksand. He was tentative and careful with each step.

His foot stuck fast with a gut wrenching squelch, the black rot gripping his ankle and his own weight making his leg sink fast. Isaac leaned back and grabbing his shin managed to pull the leg free, sans his shoe. The hole quickly folded back in on itself swallowing air, the sound of the marsh sucking into itself sounded like loose flatulence.

Isaac ran towards the nearest high rise, his feet smacking on the goo the surface tension holding briefly enough for him to pick up speed to continue. Isaac flung himself towards the thick glass of the third story window, he crashed through it careening with momentum he rolled into an office desk and came to halt in a crumpled heap.

Dazed and through blurred eyes Isaac caught the eye of the little girl cowering in the corner, her teddy bear dropped to the floor and she softly cried out of her one eye. Isaac lost consciousness before she began to scream.

———

Johnson had taken it upon himself to tend to the Cardinal's earthly vestiges himself. The prophet had deemed it unnecessary to ask for food and water so Viktor, as the Cardinal now called him, was chopping onions into a large pot of water sitting over a small stove someone had found on this rooftop garden.

Johnson had taken to wearing masks made of beauty magazines, so as to hide the fact that even his new face wasn't perfect enough. He currently was wearing the face of an ethnic woman from a nature magazine. The paper was often thin and waxy, so his spit and sweat quickly turned them to mush on his own face. This had been his twentieth mask today, bits of paper from where the onion's fumes had made him cry through the mask had become flaky and now fell into the pot of boiling water. He carried on cutting onions regardless. In the small private garden, in which someone had grown exclusively onions of all different varieties, someone had built a wooden shed filled with twenty boxes of onion bulbs and numerous tools. Viktor Johnson, knew that this was a version of happiness, a private space away from anything but onions.

The city had always prided itself on its freedom from normality where the odd wasn't shunned, and growing onions wasn't that odd in itself. When the people had stopped falling, Viktor had instructed a few of the un-ascended followers to help him clean the roof. There they had found bodies piled high enough to be spilling off the edge. After six hours they had cleared most of them, they then came across the man with the hook hand, dressed in a blood drenched onion costume. He had even tattooed his face like onion skin, Johnson, shuddered as he remembered helping push his body over side, the insides of the costume sloshing around like soup. Onion soup.

Johnson, sighed, ripped off the soggy mask and dumped the boiling soup over the side.

"There must be something else to eat in this building," he said to himself, before walking into the stairwell and descending to the Cardinals operating theatre.

It was blind. Its translucent alabaster was skin covered in tiny blue veins stretched over its empty eye sockets. White robes covered its frail frame and it could barely move beyond delicate and slow actions, as if they were caressing the air. Having all but the most rudimentary muscles removed, every turn of the head, wave of its hands and footstep was painful and strained so it choose to remain seated. Its mouth a small hole, barely enough for a straw to fit and it sighed, almost sweetly with every breath through the puckered taught maw.

Cardinal Slice sat on the floor watching it, drenched in his creation's blood and bone fragments. The Homunculus had been two people, he couldn't recall which two of his followers it had been. There had been so many that had cried and screamed so he had thrown them out the window, not unlike those that had fallen from the sky. A sacrifice to the ground. That had been the key, willingness and purity. He took their raw ingredients, shaped, stretched and moulded every facet of the physical form. Then he attached and shaved and made his flawless creation, perfection from the ugly sinful cretins that followed him. Through all the trail of pain the two acolytes had remained silent and he took what he wanted from them as it was given freely.

He reached and touched its face, which was ice cold. It let out a shudder and a single tear of blood dripped from its mouth hole.

"Do you love me?"

It breathed a slight whistle and it made Slice smile, he didn't even have to ask in the end he knew that it did. He would have spent an age gazing upon it had he not been interrupted by Viktor arriving in the elevator, dragging behind him an unconscious man.

———

A strong wind ruffled the grass at the base of the church, it stood a silent vigil at the edge of the world. The air reeked of putrefaction carried on the wind from the city. Bricks shone black and green, swimming with unknown spiritual energies.

Entities swam in and out of reality throughout the building bricks and mortar. Ghosts of potential unrealised universes, mirrored in the stained glass windows that depicted crude crucifixions of malformed creatures.

A solitary figure prayed at the feet of one such depicted creature. Her naked visage surrounded by what the artist had tried to show as ethereal light but which just was a circle of pale yellow around her hands. She was facing outwards plain and symmetrical. Ghosts swirled through the glass rippling the image making it seem like she was sharing a silent laugh at the world, a benevolent smile at the horror of the scene had been twisted to a cruel grin of malice by the passing spirits. A bright red shooting star, visible in the bright afternoon sun, arced briefly over-head, leaving a blood red scar in the sky. The sight of the star caused the ghosts to retreat from her face suddenly, the stained glass window shattered inwards coating the pile of necrotized bodies inside in shards of rainbows and lead emplacements.

The wind blew gently through the broken window and whistled through the church like the breathing of a dead man. A dead man with forgotten secrets.

———

"It never takes much to push someone over the edge, you just have to take the only thing they have, show them that it's worthless and make them throw it away for nothing," he pontificated.

Cardinal Slice was pacing back in front of Isaac throwing vulture like hand signals at him every other syllable. Casting some arcane unknown spell of anger in his direction. Viktor Johnson stood off to one to side, comforting something hidden by a sheet.

Isaac had been introduced to Johnson as he was

slapped awake by Slice from his concussive stupor. Isaac had remained silent, seething with anger at the man he had come to find.

"You don't have to justify your anguish to me, son. I've seen your pain a hundred times before," he continued.

Slice feathered his robes out behind him and took a step forward to Isaac who was sat in a plastic chair, he sneered before back handing Isaac with enough force to knock him out of the chair sideways.

"I'm the master of faith here, understand that. Through me the divine is being transmuted into existence. My knife is the rod and the carrot."

"Then why, Cardinal, are you not Pope? Rise above your lowly title, sit on the skin throne and command the others to do gods will." Isaac spat a mouthful of blood but didn't bother to move from his lying down position on the floor.

"Fool, a Pope is not a figure head. He manipulates and schemes to allow himself to remain in power and to keep his arse creases on a throne. I keep my position for my own reasons and they are no concern of yours. Oh and I have so much more to do. So many more things to make and so much blood to shed. Including yours."

Cardinal Slice walked to the back of the room and threw the sheet off his creation. The pale Homunculus screamed like knives through moist cloth from its tiny mouth. It lunged at Isaac with its black clawed hands revealing themselves from under the sleeves of its robes. Its soft movements moved at an inhuman speed and Isaac couldn't roll away fast enough as it fell atop him, scratching at his face. Its nails raked his flesh away like paper and drew blood with every swing of its hands. Yet Isaac didn't have the time raise his hands to defend himself as the weight of it pushed air from his lungs, he stared into its non-existent eyes trying to find its soul. The Homunculus began to bend forward using its tiny mouth hole to drink the blood that flowed from the many gashes in Isaac's face, holding him in place by his neck.

"It has no soul," Isaac whispered before bringing his fist up to punch its head. He connected with on the side of its head as it nonchalantly slurped, ignoring the blow. He punched twice more, on the third punch, the pale demons head began to split, the skin ripping from within by some unseen force.

It arched its back and let out a harsh whistle of pain. "You stupid creature, kill him!" Cardinal slice ran forward and began to beat the creature with a small wooden switch he had acquired from the garden upstairs. Every blow of the switch caused the creature's skin to split further and it bled black sand and glass fragments. Isaac punched it full force in its chest and it exploded in cloud of grey smoke like dust which filled the room.

Using it as cover Isaac got up and ran towards the nearest window, which he had noticed early had already been broken. Without pausing he leapt from it.

Not three stories down he landed with a soft squish into the quagmire of rotten black. He half swam half crawled away as the Cardinal watched him, all the while weeping at the loss of his first child. Yet he made the silent promise to himself to make more. Slice was determined to make them invincible. Nothing would stop him.

CHAPTER 6

The dim electric torch light finally flickered and died, leaving Fat Janet hopelessly lost in the catacombs of meat. The tunnel seemed impossibly long, the torches had only been set in the walls where she had landed as if the builders had given up and carried on in the dark. She would have retraced her steps but her muscles ached and she hadn't eaten in what seemed like forever. The sickness that came from being so hungry played tricks on her mind. She seemed to be following the smell of BBQ as it wafted through the hand dug labyrinth like some impossible and sickening prize.

"What food could be down here that wasn't made of, well, down here?" she thought.

Janet had refrained from touching or even looking at the walls since finding that fingernail, she had no choice now. Leaning against the clammy cave, Janet was sickened even more than she had been before. The wall was like mush, soft and cold like mash potato made of rot. Almost liquid, the moisture ran between her fingers. She could almost stomach the idea digging through it to escape, half swimming to the surface but her mind and stomach turned at the notion. She remembered her sinking into this tunnel to begin with, one major distur- bance could do that to every cavern in here she surmised fearfully.

The dark covered everything with a blanket of cold indifference, nothing down here mattered. All Janet had wanted was to be left alone, now here was all alone craving nothing but company and a way out.

"Fuck, is anyone down here but me!" she screamed but the walls ate every sound, hungry for syllables. Fat Janet made a decision to be silent, if she was going to starve so would this place.

Tentatively she softly patted the squishy walls and used it to guide her forwards, while each step she duly sank an inch into the muck before landing on what she continued to hope to be concrete. It occurred to Janet that she had not seen any physical sign of the city, not a car, a building or even a square foot of bubble gum ridden pavement. Janet thought that she had probably left the city a while ago. She could have been down here for days and travelled for what seemed like tens of miles.

About a year ago, she hadn't left her apartment for a span of two weeks, this was like that. No sense of time or purpose. Just walls and quiet.

Then she caught a faint odour of BBQ again, sultry and sweet, Fat Janet plodded on in desperation and to her growing horror, desperate anticipation of a cooked meal. Regardless of what it was made from.

It was a faint echo, an orgasmic moaning of a wraith

or some ethereal spectre. It chilled Janet to the bone. The tunnels had begun to thin inwards at a steady pace and Janet was now wedged sideways between the two claustrophobic layers of jellified meat, inset with the odd bleached white skull and assorted human bones.

After a few steps Janet felt the floor beneath her disappear into a pit, she stepped back but the floor slick with decay made her trip. She fell on her arse with a squelch, perched on the edge of the unseen precipice.

"Oh fuck you!" she bellowed into the seemingly infinite pit.

The pit rumbled back, a tiny roar that echoed through the walls themselves deep and unearthly.

Janet scrambled up and began to rush back through the passage she came through, the walls seemingly tighter, pressing against her. Each of her breaths seemed to push her chest into the wall, popping pockets of festering liquid hidden behind them, soaking her clothes again with rot some filth.

Janet felt forward with one hand and touched a slightly solid wall.

"No!" she exclaimed. The tunnel had been cut off. It dawned on Janet that the tunnel hadn't been dug thinner, it had shrunk of its own accord. The weight of the quickly liquefying bodies that made up the catacombs had changed the whole structure, shrinking it behind her. The roar had been the walls squashing in on themselves due to the immense pressure.

The walls pressed against Janet tighter as she struggled to get back to the pit. They began bleeding ooze as they ruptured against Janet. The ceiling began to fall against her head and Janet had to bend her neck downwards. Staring at the floor, she took a step sideways, litres of liquid ran past her feet in torrents almost knee deep instantly. Janet was blind and deaf, the rushing water fell from above her as well. The noise of the river crashing around her pierced her skull through her ears. Then there was a crack and another roar that reached the pit of her soul before the walls around her gave way and she began to drown.

Janet, helpless against the inexhaustible tide of liquid, was flushed out into the pit and she fell once again into nothing.

———

The church throbbed and ached with unseen spirits of pure magic. The ghosts that had once been drawn by such wonder had fled into the ether. Chrome sparks erupted in the air surrounding the pile of fresh bodies that glistened with a green glow and arced with blue lighting every few seconds. The electricity danced across the surfaces igniting any exposed hair of the dead with bright purple flames that danced and jittered before floating away.

The mound of broken bones and flesh throbbed and gave off an intense heat that shimmered the air itself. The stones began to bake in the heat, spotting with transformation into dull green glass.

There was a sucking sound as all the air in the church and the surrounding hill was drawn into the mound, filtering through the gaps of the bodies with small tornadoes of visible pressure, drawing the air into the sacrificial pile. A huge shock wave reverberated outwards as the universe itself fought against the happening. Space moved sideways and corrected the wrong physics of the scene. Reverberating into the past altering the normal into the obscene.

The pile of gore began to darken quickly. Black and burnt, the flesh became a cocoon and something pressed against the sides inside casting a faint outline of brilliant orange. Something born of death and glitter, something that was dreaming.

Then there was nothing, the orange glow faded and silence rang throughout the subtle holy building.

Hours passed and as the sun began to set, nothing changed as if the whole event had never occurred.

Janet awoke in a daze, she was warm and there was a soft pillow under her head. A small light flickered to her left. She rolled over, deciding that she had been an idiot to leave a candle burning on her night stand. It smelt of smoked ribs, coated in a rich glaze of sugar coated bacon.

She blinked two times in quick succession. She didn't have a scented candle like that. She always brought the ones that smelled of sea foam. Janet had never been to the seaside, ever, but she liked to imagine that she was there next to the sea eating ice cream in the late summer sunshine.

There were muffled voices and Janet's head throbbed

with pain with each word they spoke. Someone had come into view next her, the figure was kneeling down and blocked the candle light.

"Awake, eh?" It mused. "Hey, the lucky one is awake. You two come here and help get errrr her up. I'm not much good at that beyond a few errrr feet, he he."

Two flabby hands grasped her and pulled Janet into a sitting position, Janet's eyes began to focus and she looked on the rotund legless man sat in box with wheels.

"How are errrr you, eh?" he asked

"I'm ughh," Janet leaned to her side and vomited up a sizable portion of filth that she'd accidentally swallowed. "Err water, now!" the Box Man shouted to one of the people that had helped up Janet.

Janet looked around the room for the first time. The sides were made of flat steel and the floor was coated in cardboard, a fire burned in the middle and smoke drifted out a hole in the ceiling which lead out into darkness.

A large, blubbery naked person whose folds of flab covered its body, completely covered it, wobbled over to a previously unseen box in the corner, took out a bottle of water and handed it to Janet. It then handed another to the Box Man and the other figure in the corner.

The small figure was also rotund, but it was covered in red open whelps and was almost circular in shape, like a ball with eyes, arms and legs.

Janet unscrewed the lid and drank fast. She coughed and wheezed choking on the first clean water she'd had in days.

"Slow err down missy, don't want you to drown especially after what you've ever been through eh?" the Box Man said.

"Where am I?" Janet asked

"She speaks ha-ha err. Well, we're in a fridge at the moment. It's the only errrr clean place we have at the moment so we're using it as err a makeshift hospital. The fridge is under errrr well errrr I suppose you'd say ground. If you can err call corpses ground err ha-ha", said the Box Man.

"You hungry? You look hungry," the small round figure said with the voice of a child.

"I could eat a horse," Janet replied.

The whelp boy waddled awkwardly out of the fridge. "He won't be err long. We have plenty of errrr fresh ha-ha meat."

The person who had passed the water let out a long fart, it rippled up through its back flesh and escaped somewhere near its hip.

"Craig you err dirty bastard, get out and see to the crop!" said Box Man.

The thing called Craig wobbled out, giggling to itself. "You'll have to forgive Craig, the tribe think being down here for so long starts to send people err a bit daffy. Still we have plenty to share so if being daffy is err the price we pay then so be err it ha-ha."

Janet stood up and wobbled a bit uneasy on her tired feet.

"Easy, love, after that fall you had I'm errrr surprised you've not broken anything or ha-ha died."

"I know you," said Janet.

"I used to own a popular restaurant, which was errrr

well errrr I suppose it feels like a long time ago but it could have just been a few days I errrr suppose. Anyway, err, ha-ha look at me rambling, let me show you around." He wheeled himself around and with great effort pushed his box forward and out the door beckoning Janet to follow. Janet took a moment to register that these were the people from the Stuck Pig and that they didn't recognise her. Hopefully, they knew a way out. The memories of what happened in the tunnel rushed back to her all at once. Her face slackened at the thought and she knew that soon it would happen everywhere under 'ground'.

"You err coming?" the Box Man asked gently.

Janet slowly plodded forward and opened the door revealing a huge open space, dotted with fire lit torches expanding the length of a huge open space at least two hundred feet in diameter. There were about a hundred fat naked people wandering about the field carrying buckets or tending to bloody mounds growing out of the ground.

"Impressive, eh? We have a solid operation going here and we managed to organise it fairly quickly."

"What are those mounds?" Janet asked fearfully, a quiver in her voice caused by an invisible lodge slowly engorging in her throat.

"They rise out of the soil err we think they're like those that fell but from the ground. These scream something err awful though. So we take their tongues first, stop them scaring the children."

The Ball Boy waddled up to Janet from a large fire to the side where a group of people had gathered to roast pieces of meat.

He had a small plate piled high with roasted meat and offered it Janet, she started in horror at it and knocked it from his hand violently with a quick slap.

"Hey!" the boy cried.

Janet looked at the mound closest to them. It was half sticking out of the ground. Bloody and raw bits of hair poked out from the top of its head. One eye rolled around in a lidless socket the other was empty.

Its lipless mouth seemed to constantly scream as its exposed teeth clacked together noiselessly. It waved a skinless stump that should have had an arm attached, uselessly in the air like a signal flag.

Janet dry heaved her empty stomach and the Ball Boy rubbed her back in an attempt to comfort her. Janet battered him away.

"You're all wrong, so fucking wrong, what have you done?" She tried to control her heaves.

"They grow out of err the fucking earth, they are not born of woman, they are err food."

He turned his wheels to the field and motioning to one of the fat people feeding a head just poking out of the ground from a bucket.

"Err get over here for minute would you."

The fat person had slicked back black hair and the contents of its bucket sloshed as it hobbled over, Janet saw that it was the same thick black tar she was covered in. Her mind shrank, something primal screamed in her head and she ran.

"Get her, she must taste the crop. The crop is life and to deny it is errrr ha-ha death!" the Box Man shouted.

Ball Boy folded into a ball before rolling forward with

incredible speed. He careened along a few feet in a second slamming into the back of Janet's legs with enough force that she went sprawling forward a few steps. Her arms span wildly but Janet managed to keep her balance. She turned on her heel and booted the Ball Boy five feet in the opposite direction. He landed with a back spin and raced forward faster than before, a dust trail kicking up behind him. Janet deathly stepped to the side at the last moment with a quickness that surprised her. The Ball Boy carried on forwards and crashed into the side of the giant walk in fridge. His head crunched on impact and he uncurled into a small heap. His skull smashed in and his brains hanging out. Janet looked into his dead eyes as all farmers watching roared in furious unison.

Janet ran past the fridge into the darkness straight into an object. She fell over it and as she picked herself up, she realised that it was her mobility scooter, the bastards had kept it. The basket on the front was bent and broken in places but the keys were still in the ignition.

She pulled it up and clambered on. Turning the keys she pressed her foot on the accelerator. She speeded off just as the black haired farmer managed to grab the air where she had been half a second before.

Janet turned on the front light, it illuminated far into the shadows, the entire area went on for a about a mile. The grass painted white in certain places underneath meant this was the only sports field in the city. She could see remnants of skyscrapers poking into the quivering flesh roof beyond the field to her right, dimly lit by unseen sources. She turned and headed in the direction of Business Street. If she could climb up, she could get above the rot before it eventually fell on her.

There was a commotion behind her and Janet looked back at the farmers as she mounted the curb roughly. The majority of them had mounted scooters of their own, Box Man had lashed himself to the back of one behind the black haired fatty farmer with a piece of frayed rope. They all bellowed and howled murderous cries. Janet pressed onwards. Her scooter was old and didn't go that fast. They would catch up to her soon.

She turned drove past the first skyscraper and spotted robed figures wearing plain plastic masks watching from the windows. Some were spilling from the doors, all of them just watched in confusion as she rolled past. They continued to watch curiously as the twenty other mobility scooters moved to chase Janet.

Janet turned a corner into an alley too sharp and two of her wheels left the ground. She moved her weight to compensate and the wheel slammed down spinning slightly before allowing her to speed off. She smashed through dirty cardboard boxes that leapt out at her as they were illuminated in the darkness. She exited the alleyway as the first farmer entered, he managed the corner more cleanly but slower. Several other scooters crashed into the back of him. This set off the loud beeping collision alarm and the leading scooter ground to a halt, stopping the other scooters from following.

He got off and began a half-hearted fist fight with the man behind him, the black haired farmer, who was riding parallel to the now fighting farmer, wove round the ruckus and carried on forwards, dodging mouldy skulls and decaying matter lying in the street as he carried on forwards, turning at the next junction before he saw Janet speed past.

She saw him thundering down the street as she passed, the Box Man hurled insults and instructions all the while to the black haired farmer. Her scooter whined and juddered as the battery began to suddenly die. She saw the Stuck Pigs metal frame glinting off her light in the distance. She flicked the emergency switch on the back of her throttle, the small backup battery lit up and the wheels switched into four wheel drive. She would be slower but she would get there. The other scooter had turned the corner onto the same street as her and was gaining on her.

"You will taste the flesh of the earth err bitch!" Yelled Box Man chucking a bucket overhead. He misjudged his throw and it went over Janet's head splashing slick gunk on the road in front of her. Her scooter's tyres spun and thrashed on the rot, veering her to the left. Janet thrust her handle bars to the right, trying to recalibrate the tyres. The four wheel drive stopped her from buckling too much and Janet managed to correct her direction. In the meantime the black haired farmer had managed to catch up. He grabbed the back of Janet's scooter with his flabby mitt with the intent of pulling it over.

Janet reached down the side of the scooter hoping it was still there. Smiling, she grasped her walking stick and unclipped it from the side of the mobility scooter with ease. Whipping it backwards, Janet missed his hand and he began shaking Janet's scooter from right to left. Her back wheel left the ground and Janet bounced with a thud as it reconnected with the road.

She swung back again and the walking stick connected with a sharp crack. He let go with a yelp and it was responded with an insanely deep resonating growl of hatred.

The growl didn't belong to him. The ceiling began to rain thick globules of black stinking ooze. As one hit Janet's back she noticed that it was still fifty yards to the restaurant. The Box Man screamed as he looked up at roof and saw it coming undone. The massive ceiling of the meat cave began ripping open in places, waterfalls instantly falling into the chasm. There was a growing sound of an ocean in chaos and Janet looked back to see a tidal wave rising to swallow the remnants of the underground city.

She needed to go faster, there was nothing for it. Janet got off the scooter and ran faster than five miles an hour. Still clutching her walking stick she ran straight through the double doors of the Stuck Pig and slammed them shut behind her. Only stopping for a second, she caught the faintest glimpse of the Box Mann still screaming mad obscenities at her before she slammed the door shut and locked the dead bolts into position.

"Please kill me," came a soft voice behind her.

Janet turned and screamed in abject horror at the worst thing she'd seen that day.

The black cocoon throbbed and buckled. A loud thumping came from within. After each thump a small portion of the black crust crumbled off. After the tenth thump a crack appeared splitting down the side. Pale blue and intense light shone out of the gap and plumes of red smoke seeped out. There was another thump as the creature inside bashed against its cage.

The cracks spread like a web across the surface with every thump, the black crust of the egg began to completely fall away. All at once it exploded outwards in an array of black dust and crimson mist.

Out of the fog slowly walked a naked woman, her skin glittering purple, blue and green. She smiled softly and crouched down picking up a pile of the black dust.

She played with it, passing it from hand to hand. Then she blew a lungful of air into it, scattering it in a cloud of white hot fire.

The fire blew from her hands like a blowtorch and she scorched words into the walls of the church.

She stopped the flames, arched her back and laughed at her handiwork in a melancholy chuckle that was almost a thin whisper. The words read "Glitterwitch."

CHAPTER 7

I saac clung onto the metal structure. The unruly tide of black water rushed past threatening to take him with it. He watched a skull idly float past, its empty sockets echoing how he felt.

He had fallen from the building after his fight with that, thing, and managed to make it here back to where it had started. This stupid giant mascot, so dented that its friendly smile was twisted and bent beyond anything sane. It seemed to Isaac like a cruel smirk, the statue mocking his failure to keep to his promise, to finish the job he had started.

That bastard Slice had been right there. He looked so weak and easy to finish. It was too late now. He wrapped his arm tighter round the support beam and looked for a foot hole or a ladder of some kind. He had been swimming in it for about a day resting where he could. Eventually the currents had become too strong and he found his way to the bowler hat of Cracklin.

He was in abject despair and had reached the point

of giving up and letting himself drown beneath the black waves. Then he heard voices, echoing through the steel hat. One of them he recognized as Janet.

———

The restaurant was in a state. Dark blood stains covered pretty much everything, the troughs had been overturned and the counter that the till had rested on had been knocked onto its side and by the smell had been used as a toilet.

She was hanging from a makeshift crucifix. The troughs had been nailed to the wall like a cross and she was tied by the belly to them. Her intestines had spilled from a gaping, festering wound in her belly. She had one end of them in her mouth constantly chewing on herself.

Janet recognised her as the woman who had her kicked out here the first time. She was still pale and waterlogged, yet somehow she looked more alive. Her face was an expression of constant pain, yet still she chewed.

"I'm, so hungry all the time. Don't judge me, please, they left me as an example of what greed is. I'm so famished, I need to eat."

Janet looked at her face and the brown spittle that leaked down her chin had stained most of dress. Janet noticed that her teeth had been filled down to points, short needles constantly chewing. She swallowed a mouth full of intestine and spat a lump of faeces out the side of her maw, it landed with a splat next to a pile of what Janet realised was the woman's own shit.

"Kill me, please?" she said pleadingly. Her eyes darted to a clean cleaver that lay some feet from Janet. Janet found herself torn between sympathy and disgust, how was this woman not dead.

"How are you not dead?" Janet repeated her thoughts, asking not the woman but to herself.

"I don't know, nobody dies anymore."

"That's ridiculous."

The woman swallowed and spat again.

"Check there, under the table. There's proof of what I'm saying. I'm so sorry in advance at the state of it, I needed to eat and it was fresh."

Janet's hands trembled as she picked up the plywood table. It was clean and the smell underneath wasn't shit and piss. It was rotting meat. She tossed the table aside and gasped aloud. There, lying by itself was a half-eaten set of lungs connected to a malformed trachea. The right one had been bitten into but the left was intact. It was green and black, putrefaction had begun to set in yet it was clearly still alive. It silently wheezed inwards by itself, pumping breath into itself, the hole filled lung farting like a whoopee cushion with each inhale, sucking in more air with every exhale. With every second exhale, droplets of yellow phlegm dripped out the throat hole, dripping out at regular intervals.

Janet screamed out loud and let the table drop back onto them with a squelch.

"You see, its madness. Once we realised that we couldn't die and, well, the idea came to me that I had all the food I could ever want. In me. I made the hole in my belly and they tried to stop me. They tied me up here and left to find actual meat. A proper meal, they said."

"You asked me to kill you, yet you said you can't die."
"Cut out my brain and chop it into mush. I won't be me anymore, in a sense. I won't know I'm alive. Please, do this for me."

"I, I can't. I don't have it in me. I'm no murderer." the woman let the intestines fall from her mouth. They dropped, dragging the rest of them downwards. They snaked outwards and uncoiled like a slimy rope onto the floor.

"You coward," the watery woman said smiling evilly. "You come to my house and don't follow my rules. I would have you cast out but you will look better on my plate."

She reached down and ripped the ropes tying her to the cross as if they were paper. Dropping down into a crouch she scooped her guts up and half-heartedly pushed them back inside herself with a grunt.

"It would have been easier to fall on you from up there. Jelly's much better eating, don't you know!"

Her jaw unhinged and her mouth grew two feet wider, snarling she leapt forward in an impossible leap for someone of her size. Intending to swallow Janet whole.

A large chunk of metal collided with the malformed woman's head halfway into her leap, making her mistime her jump missing Janet by a hair's breadth.

"Janet quickly!" she turned and saw Isaac, soaked through with rot, standing by the kitchen entrance.

"I'll devour you both!" the Blob Woman shouted, quickly getting to her feet,

Janet swung the walking stick she just remembered she still held overhead, the handle fell downwards and Janet meant to stave in the Blob Woman's head. The blow was softly absorbed by the Blobwoman's face flab. Janet swung again and split the skin. The Blob Woman's eyes rolled back into her head unconscious. She went to swing again, raising the walking stick far above her head when Isaac grabbed it firmly and looked into her eyes.

Janet looked back towards the door, the noise outside was deafening. Then like a thunder crack in the night, the door smashed open inwards. The tide of black decay smashed into all three of them. They swirled and barrelled over each other, powerless against the force. Janet held onto the walking stick for dear life and Isaac reached to grab her other arm fruitlessly.

After what was only seconds, yet seemed like hours to them, they crashed into the far wall, the pressure of the incoming torrent filled the room almost instantly. The bricks around the door had shot out like bullets after the door had given way, the frame disintegrated immediately taking the side of the building with it.

Isaac let out a gasp of bubbles and tried to surface but the water's weight kept him down. Feeling something finally he grabbed a hold of an arm, Janet's arm. He tried to pull her up but Janet was seemingly knocked out from the impact.

Isaac let go and swam to the ceiling but found that the room was full to the brim. He began to panic when he felt a tug on her leg. Janet was still awake, she moved up to his arm and together they managed to feel their way to the kitchen door, it had also been destroyed by the incoming rush of the water, and the stainless steel hinges had been ripped clean off.

Isaac led Janet to the ladder he had used to descend. The kitchen was pitch black and by memory and sheer luck he found the still intact ladder. They used it haul themselves clear of the black water. Gulping huge gasps of air they then began climbing their way out of the pit of undeath underneath the waves, to light, to escape, to another hell.

CHAPTER 8

A ngels. He had crafted his own heavenly peons. Pale and strong, they would fly and carry his message to his willing disciples from this roof across the city, slashing his words into the flesh of anyone regardless of if they had taken up his mantel, sigils and robes of his order.

Cardinal Slice was a god and he stood in the presence of twenty new Homunculi, each eight feet tall, lithe and winged. They fluttered with anticipation and stood naked on the precipice of the balcony, their clawed talons gripping the concrete railing. Cardinal Slice stood naked, covered in dried blood. He gestured to the flooded city, with only the tallest buildings breaking through the filthy, black water. The surface swallowing any light from the blinding sun.

Johnson stood back from Slice, his current magazine mask depicting a blender after confusing one of Cardinal Slices rants about conventional beauty beyond the human body. Bold comic sans font that he had ripped off to make the mouth hole, would have read 'Ten speed strawberry massive!" the slogan offended him but he didn't know why.

The Homunculi breathed in unison, dry and raspy and Viktor Johnson was reminded of tearing paper being eaten by beaked monstrosities from some long forgotten nightmare. Johnson knelt and the crowd behind him did the same, one hundred robed acolytes silent and awestruck.

"My beloved ones." Slice addressed his creations and then turned to his followers. "My treasured followers, we have but one goal left to us, spurn the unbelievers and kill them. Soon we all will be as my angels." He turned back around.

"My Beauties, fly, kill, and convert. Be the best of yourselves."

Silently the Homunculi flapped their leathery wings and rose into the air. They took off heavily, each flap of their wings beating huge gusts of wind against Cardinal Slice and his acolytes. They lifted up higher until they were pinpricks of black against the blue sky.

Victor Johnson was passed a spare robe by a follower behind him, which he in turn put on the Cardinal.

The masked followers made their way down into an empty conference room. Victor hung back as to speak with the Cardinal.

"Johnson, select some followers for enlightenment would you? We need to expand and fast, too many ugly people in this city wallowing about unchecked. Perfection means one hundred percent of them must be angels or nothing, don't forget that."

The masked followers milled in the conference room a floor below the roof level. There, they slept and chatted, but mostly they huddled in confusion. Those creatures were not the beauty they had been promised, they looked nothing like the people that fell from the sky. Ten minutes passed and Johnson followed them down, instructing two small children and an adult to follow him back upstairs. Silence followed as the followers listened to the mumbled shouting from above them. Then the screams began lasting for hours on end.

Johnson returned after they fell silent again and looked at them. His mask was stained with blood and his eyes were hollow, dead from the outside in. He had never seen the transformation process before then and it terrified him to the core. He walked to the window and looked out. There he spotted the man from earlier climbing into the giant statue of the pig. Johnson knew that he had some connection to the Cardinal, some unknown rage boiled inside him and Johnson decided that he had to know why Slice was this way, so twisted and intent on perverting people, so focused on pain. Perhaps he would know, know enough to stop him or at least enough to cripple him so he could kill him and end this.

Janet reached the top of the ladder, struggling to pull herself out of the water on to the steel struts of Cracklin's bowler hat. It was the only non-skyscraper building above the flood. Isaac pushed her from underneath and she managed to flop onto the side which he quickly dropped onto himself.

Janet dropped her knees and let out a piercing scream of frustration whilst her hands shook like jack hammers. "Oh god, oh my fucking god Isaac. They were growing out of the ground, the greedy fucks, peeling them like bananas, blood, and darkness everywhere. Isaac you bastard you let me fall, why didn't you grab me? I can't I need to clean be clean. I need a fucking pizza. Oh god, Isaac, why, fucking why, they can't die, we can't die. Fuck why, oh my god why?"

Isaac put his arm around Janet and she shrugged it off instantly. Isaac backed off, feeling unsure he didn't know what to do or say. He lent against the curve of the bowler hat, on a section that wasn't dented and watched the water flow and ebb. He noticed it was making waves like an actual sea.

Janet continued to sob and scream for hours and Isaac's guilt grew with each tear she shed.

Eventually the sun began to set and Janet fell quiet and asleep out of sheer exhaustion. Isaac lay down next to her trying to fall asleep himself. He needed to find a way out of this, he needed help and Isaac had only one place that had helped him before. Helped him get passed the murder of his husband. He needed to find a church.

He and Janet needed to get to a church. There would be answers there. Hopefully.

————

Johnson had told the sheep to go upstairs one at a time, once an hour and they did. This would give him time away from Slice and his needs.

He had found a bunch of big empty water cooler bottles and thick packaging tape in a storage cupboard and had fashioned a crude boat, managing with some effort to lower it out one of the larger windows into the water. He had a backpack on filled with as many dried cereal bars and small water bottles as he could carry.

He was about to leap from the window into the water when an acolyte called him with a voice like oiled gravel.

"Johnson, the Cardinal declares you are to be next." Johnson sighed. He needed the Cardinal to be distracted. If he sent those, things after him, he wouldn't last two minutes.

"Fine I'm coming give me two minutes to get a fresh mask, eh?"

"He said if I didn't bring you personally, I wouldn't ascend myself," explained the disciple.

"You want to become one of those things?"

"We're already them, his hands and our suffering make it possible in this realm."

"You want to suffer?"

"Is this a test? We do as we are begat. You told me that, Mr. Johnson, those are your words."

"I could have been wrong."

"We have no choice now, look outside. The tar rises Mr. Johnson and we need to fly like angels. Don't test my faith."

"You're right, you're so right but, I'm not worthy, I'm just a poor old midget with a gammy leg and no crutch. I'm weak, I have not suffered enough to transform. You though, you're ready, aren't you?"

"I am."

"Here take this then," Johnson took off his blender mask and handed it to the acolyte who took off its plain plastic one. Underneath the acolyte was a bald, olive skinned woman, her lower jaw was twisted downwards and her mouth hung open, lopsided and drooling. She gave him an embarrassed look and quickly put the mask on, looping the hairy string behind her ears.

"You are Johnson now, go be with your suffering and let it change you to who you know you are."

She rushed forward and hugged him warmly. He patted her on the back twice and watched as she left. Johnson reached in his backpack and pulled out his shotgun. The stock had been sharpened like a spear to a crude point. He would need it soon, if Slice didn't fall for his ruse.

These people were stupid and deserved everything they had coming to them, Johnson had no qualms about leaving them behind.

With that thought echoing in his head, he jumped from the window and splashed into the ocean. He went under briefly before rising again and climbing aboard his raft, his weapon still in hand. The Sun began to set and he paddled towards the steel bowler hat.

———

S lice beckoned the non-Johnson closer with his hand without looking directly at her. He stood in the middle of the roof watching the fading light of day reflect off the glass in the next building. The windows painted a pale orange with the fading light.

"You've been very patient, but you're going to have to wait longer. You're not ready yet, you may never be ready to have your soul travel into the new body you have, but you can take me and others there when they have to. You hear what I'm saying? Do you understand, Vicktor? I will teach you everything you'll need to know to."

Slice turned around and saw not Johnson, he was taken aback slightly.

"Where is he?" he calmly asked the acolyte.

"He's gone, I'm the new Johnson. He bequeathed me the title. I'm ready to become me."

He heard the sloshing of something beneath him and turned back around to see Johnson awkwardly paddling with his hands away from the building.

"My dear take off that idiotic mask."

She did and Slice turned back around and flinched at her disfigurement.

"Johnson, hmm?"

"Yes, your worship."

"Go and fetch me five more of my followers, we will need a mighty beast to quench the treachery in his heart with fire. They will be a beautiful Wurm and together we'll vanquish him and his conspirators."

"Conspirators?" a thin strand of clear spit leaked from her mouth, she didn't clean it away out of fear.

"Do you know my title, my dear?"

"C, Cardinal."

"You do have a brain, excellent. Yes, do you know what's above a Cardinal? No, don't answer your maw dribbles something disgusting when you talk. The answer is the Pope." He said the last word with restrained vigour. "I killed the Pope. You don't get to be the Pope by killing him, but you do get to silence him, so we will silence Vicktor and those that have poisoned him against us. Go fetch me raw materials and willing minds. We have a few limp dogs to put down."

He waved her away with a motion and continued to watch his ex-servant paddle to the steel platform. Then he watched as two figures in the distance wrestled him to the ground. He smiled slightly as a punch was connected. He would have to work quickly, Vicktor was his kill not theirs.

Whomever they were.

———

"No please, I just..."

Isaac punched him again and the squirming little man's nose crunched harshly. A jet of blood squirted out and splashed Isaacs's already dirty face.

"You piece of shit. Tell me where he is? Does he have more of those things?" Isaac's blood boiled with anger as he screaming into the dwarfs face.

"My nose, you broke it. Awwgh."

"I'll do more than that, tell me!"

"Yes, he has at least twenty of them now. They're flying around the city now, killing anything not them, he's killing his own people he told me this," Johnson made a noise when he breathed in. "Gnn," he breathed again as Isaac stared into his eyes, looking for the truth.

"They don't have eyes, how do they know?"

"They wouldn't, I suppose, think about it Isaac they'll just destroy everything," said Janet slowly. She was stood off to one side her face was blank and she just stared into nothingness.

"She's... wrong, they know, he controls them. They believed in him before they became those things, that's real power."

"Where is he, where is that butcher? That Psychopath?"

"Behind gnn you, that building. He's watching us right now probably. We need to gnn go, those winged horrors, with gnn thick black talons please."

"He has a boat, Isaac we can just float away," Said Janet dreamily.

"Fine. You're coming with us, if he catches us maybe we can use you as a shield."

Isaac got up off Johnson and wrenched him to his feet, then pushed him forward onto the boat made of empty water dispenser bottles and brown tape. Isaac and Janet clambered aboard and pushed off from the side of the bowler hat and paddled them away towards the last light of the sun as it blinked behind the horizon.

"Have you got any food?" asked Janet.

"Gnn... in my bag. Please, help yourself," replied Johnson sarcastically.

Janet opened up the backpack and took out the shotgun. She casually tossed it over the side with a soft plop. "Gnn we needed that to defend ourselves! You've probably gnn killed us now."

"You could have used it on us at some point, its better off out of the picture," said Janet as she opened one of the cereal bars and mindlessly chewed on it.

"Any water?" asked Isaac.

Janet threw him a bottle and he half drained it in a second. He looked at Johnson with darted eyes and then offered it to him. Johnson denied it with a shake of his head.

"Listen gnn, how do you know the Cardinal?" "He killed my husband and many others. Before all this. They were placed under his care and he murdered them in some twisted desire to become the Pope."

"Jeez, that gnn sounds horrible and utterly insane. Was your husband important?"

"To me he was important but no, the church didn't do anything about the Cardinal until he killed one of their own. Then all they did was bring him here. So he was out their way."

"That's it? He's not a god? He didn't bring the people from the sky, he can't control them?"

"I don't know, he's a fucking nutjob and I came here to kill him."

Janet stayed silent, realising she knew nothing about Isaac. He scared her how he spoke of killing so easily.

"Are those fingers on your face real then, Isaac?" asked Janet.

Isaac smiled coyly. He went over and sat next to Janet leaving Johnson to paddle by himself.

"I'm sorry for not telling you, Janet." He put his arms around her and held her tight. Janet stayed static, not reciprocating the embrace. Isaac held her for half a minute before letting go.

"No, they're not real." Isaac said peeling the rubber finger and thumbs off his face and throwing them into the water.

"Is there a church nearby?" Isaac asked.

"Gnn yes, about five miles away. I mean it used to be there, it's probably underneath this stuff by now," replied Johnson.

"Let's find out, can't hurt," mumbled Janet through a mouthful of cereal.

Beneath the waves in the dark a hand caught the shotgun and another grabbed the rubber fingers before letting them both go and sink slowly downwards. A hundred more hands attached to naked bodies swam through the darkness to the surface. Following the ripples the makeshift boat made through the water.

CHAPTER 9

The Glitterwitch waved her hand and summoned rainbow cupcakes out of the air. They sat on a plain white plate. She sat on one of the remaining pews she hadn't carefully changed into something more comfortable and took a bite out one of them. They were perfect. The frosting changed flavour every ten seconds, this bite was peanut butter which turned into vanilla by the time she swallowed. She was in her own personal heaven.

Struck by an idea, she stepped up and walked out the church. The hill was lit by the stars and the moon, as eerie and calm as the graveyard she stood in, as if something else unnatural besides herself was happening. "This won't do at all," she said, her mouth still full of cake. She exhaled a plume of yellow feathers and they swished and morphed into a thousand little canaries. The canaries circled the church and flew around it. The church began to grow and morph. The ghosts of the church began to flee from their hiding places in the bricks and leaked out into the hill. The ground shone green in places as they were exorcised from the building. The Glitterwitch laughed and danced as they swam around the grass, purposefully avoiding her. Spinning in circles, she marvelled as the grass sprouted poppies where she stepped. She stopped spinning for a moment and plucked one, it shimmered like she did purple and green. The Canaries flew faster and faster, becoming a yellow blur in the cold light of moon. Time began to unwind backwards. The broken glass rose from the ground and reformed itself in the windows. The bricks cleaned themselves, no longer old and grey with dead moss, they were clean, red and blunt.

Then the canaries flew away into the night and as they disappeared over the horizon, the Glitterwitch saw her own reflection in the stain glassed window. It wasn't a reflection though just a perfect representation of her face made of cut pieces of glass.

She smiled and the window smiled back.

"That's better," she said, before going back inside to finish her cupcakes.

———

Slice pulled his replacement Johnson aboard the pallid, grey skinned and sweaty back of the beast. Its sharp, obsidian, black teeth bared beneath lipless gums rested in front of its short neck and elongated skull. Its five exposed brains on the back of its head hummed with electricity and hatred. Its ten foot longs wings twitched nervously as it hunched on all four of its sharpened talon lined claws. Its eye sockets were hollow, dark pit's leading to the inside of its skull and its grey skin was taught and leather like.

"My dear, what's your name?"

"Johnson," she replied.

"No, you'll not have a failure's name, a rat's name.

I'll call you, ha-ha, after the old Pope."

He took her hand and wrapped it around his waist. "Wagstaff, you're Wagstaff, yes?"

"Yes, Cardinal."

He grinned, his perfect white teeth showing. "Watch this," he said, pressing his fingers into one the exposed brains on the back of the Dragon's head. It roared with pain and he laughed long and maddeningly. Above them hovered twenty new Homunculi, each looking dead and pallid in the night, spectral, bat like figures of death. None of his followers in the building remained. Cardinal Slice had transformed all of them into his perfect army.

"Now, fly!" he screamed, thrusting his fingers into the brains. The Homunculi-Dragon breathed a cone of arcane white hot fire, gave an earth-shattering high pitched cry and flapped its wings. After three beats of them it slowly took off. Wagstaff clung on for dear life and as they flew higher. She leant over the side and vomited onto the now shrinking roof of the building.

Cardinal slice looked back at her.

"Disgusting. You'll have to redeem yourself, child."

"Yes, your benevolence."

He continued to grin cruelly and steered the Dragon towards the rising moon, towards the direction he saw them paddle off in. The Homunculi followed at first, before quickly over taking him and the Dragon. Smelling prey they grew impatient, hungry for their first kill.

———

J anet spotted the first Homunculi as they left the city boundary by the light of the moon. Passing by the last skyscraper in the city, only the top floor was visible by internal candle light. They could also see the cultists watching them pass silently from the windows and the roof top.

Janet pointed to the roof as a dark object descended on the cultists, diving into them picking them up one by one and dropping them into the water. She gasped in abject horror at the sight. Isaac and Johnson stood agape watching the spectacle of death as the cultists landed in the water, quickly disappearing under the black tide. The acolytes screamed and rushed into the lower floors to escape but the dark objects descended en masse, breaking through the windows and tearing them apart.

One of the Homunculi flew towards their boat and Janet finally screamed.

Isaac tackled her to the floor as it went to grab her head. It flew past, its talons clacking against themselves as it missed her by a clear foot.

Janet got her first clear look at the warped creation and it terrified her so much she temporarily forgot about the horrible things she saw beneath the meat earlier that day.

"Oh fuck gnn this!" said Johnson as he began to paddle with renewed vigour.

The Homunculi turned and tried for another dive. It raced down with supernatural speed and Isaac managed to throw himself and Janet into the water to avoid it. It had compensated for this and grasped onto Janet's shoulders carrying her from the water for several feet. She reached up and dug her nails into its calves. It breathed out in pain as Janet tore into its paper like skin. The muscles became quickly exposed as she drew its black sand like blood and it dropped her in its pain.

Janet landed in the water with a splash and disappeared under the waves.

The Homunculi flew off back towards the tower, back towards easier prey.

"Janet!" Isaac yelled looking over to where she went under. He dived into the water. Instantly blinded and deafened by the black ink, he surfaced as quickly as he could. "Janet!" he cried out again. Isaac saw nothing but the waves gently moving with the current. Suddenly, she surfaced two feet to his right, coughing up water and the remains of her last cereal bar.

"Fuck, we need to get back to the boat Isaac," she said after a few seconds.

"No, it's too big a target for those things."

"You don't understand, they're in the water. They're gonna pull us down with them."

Isaac and Janet looked towards the boat. It had travelled quite a distance away, despite Johnson's pathetic paddling. Johnson had carried on going out of pure fear.

"You stop that boat, you fucker!" yelled Janet, Vicktor Johnson ignored them. He wasn't going to die. Not after everything he'd been through.

"I'm sorry gnn," he whispered to them. He never used to be a coward but it had stopped him dying before, it was who he was now.

Janet and Isaac gave up trying to swim after the boat, Johnson had travelled too far.

A mighty roar pierced the night and the huge form of Slice's dragon swooped through the cloud of the Homunculi, crashing into the building, taking most of the roof with it. It took off and swooped around perching itself on the edge of the hole it had just made facing into it. The windows of the top floor exploded outwards as white hot fire burst throughout it, turning any remaining occupants to ash, cultists and Homunculi all. The fire continued to burn, illuminating the surrounding ocean like it was day.

It took off again after a few flaps of its massive wings, Isaac and Janet watched in awe as it flew overhead. It breathed fire onto the boat melting it instantly. Johnson managed to leap away just in time.

He surfaced above the water for a few seconds, struggling to tread water with a bad leg. He lived his last few seconds in a blind panic before the dragon swooped down with its massive jaws and bit into him. It hovered two feet above the water chewing his bones and flesh for a few seconds before letting the top half of his tattered and bloody torso drop into the water. He sank this time.

Slice whooped in triumph and looked around for anyone else. Wagstaff was crying pure terror.

"Those were your followers! They loved you!" she cried, lamenting the deaths of those in the skyscraper.

"It doesn't matter. They were not perfect like me or my creations! All that are not will be destroyed!"

He then flung her off the back off the Dragon with his right arm into the water.

"Now you join them!" he bellowed, pulling at the Dragon's brains. It turned and reached down to kill her as it had done with Johnson.

The water around the Dragon began to seethe with bubbles and movement. A hundred naked beautiful people leapt from the water with inhuman speed. Lithe, well-toned bodies of men, women and androgynous people without genitals began crawling onto its body. Swarming all over it, they tore it to shreds, each one biting and ripping huge sections of flesh out of it with their bare hands.

The Dragon thrashed in pain and Slice was thrown from it into the water as the Dragon tried to take off. A hugely muscled and long haired woman coated in the black slime of the water clambered up onto it's one of its wings. She pulled the membrane of the wing apart with her incredible strength, throwing huge sections of it over her shoulder into the water.

The Dragon crashed into the water, causing a huge wave to cascade outwards. Janet and Isaac had been treading water the whole time but were pulled under the water as it passed over their heads. They surfaced together to see the naked people continue to drag the Dragon under the waves, it's head let out one last plume of fire before succumbing to their relentless attack and sinking beneath the pitch black.

Wagstaff screamed one last time as she also was pulled underneath by them.

The naked people began surfacing themselves one by

one, popping their heads out of the water, laughing and splashing each other like this was some sort of game.

Janet began tugging her sodden and torn clothes off in panic.

"Quick! They might think we're one of them!" She motioned to Isaac and they both quickly managed to strip whilst treading water.

The beautiful people stopped frolicking and began swimming towards the on fire skyscraper, ignoring Janet and Isaac as they passed. Thousands of them began crawling up every surface of the building. The remaining Homunculi swarmed around and began diving at them ripping them from the sides. Every now and again a person would grab one of their legs and drag a Homunculus down into the water to never been seen again.

Eventually, the crowd reached the top and began screaming at a harsh pitch. Each one achieved a tone higher than a human should be able to produce. Isaac and Janet began to swim away from them as the Homunculus stopped their attacks.

The Homunculus hearts exploded out of their torsos, leaving massive gaping wounds in their chests. Quickly afterwards they fell from the sky crashing into the water, being dragged underneath the waves by the naked people as Slice's followers had done so before.

Janet and Isaac reached the unconscious form of Cardinal Slice floating upside down. Isaac managed to flip him onto his back and strip his clothes from him. A single empty bottle that had been part of the boat floated past and Isaac and Janet grasped onto it. Isaac with one hand and the other he kept a hold of Slice, who he hoped was still alive. The good Cardinal had much to atone for and Isaac wasn't going to let him off easily. He would answer for what he did before Isaac would throttle him.

They floated off in the opposite direction to the now rising sun, away from the city, the burning building and most of all towards the tiny dot of a building in the distance. The tiny speck that was the church on Green Hill.

CHAPTER 10

A Year Ago.
Isaac stood soaked in his kilt at the pearl marble altar. Gordon stood opposite. They smiled and kissed, the church crowd applauded. Their matching gold rings were inscribed with the personal love note. "Love forever strong."

Eight Months ago
"Is he okay?" Isaac couldn't stop sobbing. The Doctor shook his head and offered some form of condolences. Gordon would live but he would never be normal again, confined to a bed completely mute and unable to move a muscle. Isaac would never see his husband smile again.

. . .

Seven *months ago.*
"We of the Church of the Flesh can guarantee that we can get him not only moving normally again but have his face back to its beautiful self." said the priest from the other side of the confession booth. The thin grill set in repeatable shapes of scalpels separated Isaac from him.

"Please, whatever it takes, I need the best. I have plenty of money," pleaded Isaac.

"Well a sizeable donation might swing things in your favour. We have a visit from the Cardinal next week we might be able to get him to do the service."

"Yes, anything."

A small credit card machine popped out of the wall. "Please enter your pin number," the priest said calmly.

Five *months ago.*
It was a surprisingly sunny day everywhere but in Isaac's heart. He threw the pile of dirt into the grave. The coffin was a tasteful whalebone colour. Gordon's favourite. He chugged back a swig from his flask and turned away from his husband's grave. Making his way through the small crowd he avoided attempts to console him. He only felt despair and hatred. He only wanted what was fair, revenge.

. . .

F *our and half months ago.*
        "Dude, it's fully loaded and for you, it's pro bono. Anyone willing to take down a Pope killer is a friend to me." The hooded man slid the package over the bar table to Isaac.

"Thank you, sir," said Isaac, pocketing it.

"Exile, can you believe it? The fucker botched a simple nose job and the Pope bled to death. A fucking Cardinal should have known better. He did it on purpose. Accident, my arse."

"I don't care, that's not my reason for this."

"Hey, dude, as long as you're going to do it."

"No one will stop me."

T *wo months ago.*
        Fat Janet was halfway through a quadruple pizza tower, stroking her cat Puddin' Pop between bites. There was a commotion outside her window. She got up out of her sticky leather chair and looked out.

A police man with no ears was arresting some normie. "You tourists are not allowed firearms in this city, too many trophy hunting sick fucks coming here. You understand only citizens who pass the ugly test can carry guns. " the policeman was calmly explaining the situation to the man.

"Please I need this, he's here, and I know it. I need to kill him!" the man was screaming insanely.

The policeman looked up directly at Janet and she stepped away and closed the curtain.

"None of my business," she said, shooing Puddin Pop away from her pizza stack.

She was pretty sure that crazy man would be in jail before the hour was out.

A week ago.
The homeless man was eating the remains of some mash potato out of a bin. Greedily slurping it down. Something hard was pressed into his back.

"I have you now!"

There was a loud shot as the gun was fired. The homeless man crumpled to the ground in a lifeless heap. Isaac looked down at him. It was not Slice. Isaac had murdered an innocent homeless man. He'd been lied to.

He threw the gun in the same bin the homeless man had been eating out of and ran as far away from the scene as he could. The fake finger and thumb hanging from his cheek wobbled as fast as his feet moved.

CHAPTER 11

The morning was misty, cold and clammy. The black tide smashed against the side of the church, staining the grey bricks with its awful smell and corrosive touch.

Janet and Isaac half dragged Cardinal Slice through the mud of the shallow quagmire that now covered the hill.

"Is he really worth all this effort? We could have just left him to die," said Janet grunting with effort.

"The things he's done are too much. He needs to swear his guilt in front of those he betrayed and seek forgiveness. Then I'll kill him, it's the only way."

Janet remained quiet as they climbed the slippery stone steps to the church's untouched gnarled oak doors and with some effort they dragged him inside. The church was relatively untouched. A skylight had been smashed open by something unseen, the pews coated in thick layer of ash and dust as if untouched for years.

They dropped Slice with a clump, his muscles clapping against the stone cobbles of the church's floor.

Isaac went to close the doors, taking one last look at the fog covered ocean that covered what seemed like the entire world. Then he saw something come running towards the church out of the water.

"Janet, get out the way!" he shouted, barrelling himself to the side of the doors. A huge, watery mass of a person smashed through them, screaming madness before stopping in front of the naked Slice.

The Blobwoman's head was caved in, exposing her brain and her one remaining eye whipped around with madness before settling on Janet. A thick strand of drool dripped from her unnatural mouth and she went to step over the Cardinal. Before her foot hit the floor it was grasped and harshly pulled backwards by the surprisingly strong grip of Slice.

The Blobwoman fell at an angle, smashing face first into one of the pews. The wood splintered under the impact and a huge splinter stuck fast through her empty eye socket and out of the opening in the back of the Blob Woman's head.

There she lay permanently paralyzed.

Slice got up and made a show to pat non-existent dust off his frame. He then peered into the brain of the woman. "Hmm, I've seen this damage before. No return from that of course only course of action is a mercy killing. Which I won't give, I'm done with those."

"Slice!" screamed Isaac from behind him.

Slice looked up and winked at Janet, then he turned to face Isaac.

"You again. Very disappointing to see you're still alive. I must try harder with my next creations."

"There's no one left but you, madman. You turned everyone into those things."

"No," said Janet softly, "no one can die now, they just rot and become the sea outside."

Slice looked passed Isaac through the open doors to the ocean. The fog had cleared somewhat and the morning sun sparkled off the black surface like diamonds.

"The water is always pretty this time of day but far from my vision of beauty. It's unfinished," replied Cardinal Slice.

"Shut up, you owe me, Slice, you owe me your death," said Isaac.

"Didn't you hear her, you grieving buffoon? Nobody dies anymore." Slice turned and motioned with one of his hands to the now twitching body of the Blobwoman. "But we break."

Slice quickly grabbed the splinter of wood out of the woman's skull and with a sickening slurp pulled it free. He then hurled the sizable chunk of wood like a spear at Janet. It stopped in mid-air a few meters in front of Janet's face, floating unnaturally.

The Glitterwitch descended from the ceiling. She was bathed in a red glow of pure otherworldly fury and she floated a few feet from the ground between Isaac and Slice. "You all have trespassed in my home, bringing pain and suffering. This is shameful and brings anger upon my threshold. Be gone."

The red glow covered the entire church. The pews rattled back and forth echoing her words. The splinter trembled with unseen force and flew backwards into Slice's own head. He gargled a few nonsense words as blood squirted from the wound and fell backwards. He remained alive but brain dead, staring at the ceiling and making sucking noises like his own creations.

The Glitterwitch floated over to him and stared deep into his thoughtless mind with her own.

"A mercy killing indeed," she screamed in a voice so high pitch it was silent. Cardinal Slice breathed his last breath and his chest exploded outwards in a rain of gore before he went totally slack.

The Glitterwitch turned to the trembling Janet and pointed to her.

"You, thin pretty girl. You shall be the seed of this moment. I stopped death, I made myself, I gave the world unlimited beauty and it was sullied by you and your kind. You spoiled my gifts."

Janet began to cry as she fell to her knees. "I just want a pizza, this is not my fault."

"Hmpf it's as much your fault as it was the surgeon's, as it was the grieving husband's, as it was the crippled coward's, as it was the greedy whore's! I was supposed to be nice and pure. Now look at me, hating, and killing! No more!"

The church began to morph and twist, the brick walls becoming long, thin, snarling mouths full of dulled yellow teeth which were snapping at nothing. The roof opened up to reveal the sky full of fire and raining ash. The ocean outside solidified into sand then into black obsidian mid wave, sharp beautiful fingers reaching towards the church.

A ball of dancing light materialised above the Glitter-witch and with a wave of her hand it was flung towards Isaac.

He ignited instantly. Screaming in agony, his skin blackened and his nerves popped with the extreme heat. In his last seconds of life Isaac's final thoughts were of his soaked suit at his wedding and the feeling of grave dirt in his hand. Then with a blinding light he was incinerated instantly.

"NO!" Janet screamed seeing her only friend die in a second.

"He couldn't forgive Janet. He was bereft of love of truth, I just destroyed his lifeless husk. There was no soul left in that man."

"That's not true! He rescued me more times than I should have been saved, he loved me."

The Glitterwitch laughed.

"You are deluded, yet I feel in your love. Selfish and small but it's there. Perhaps you're worth saving, worthy of his actions, although perhaps not. You have lost hope. A mercy killing would be better. With this word, I make it so everything can die again. I take back my mercy from the world and give it to you."

Another fireball appeared over her head again, Janet closed her eyes and waited to burn just like Isaac had.

There came a sound of flapping wings suddenly from behind the Witch. A Homunculus had crawled out of the ocean and moved silently behind her until it spoiled its presence with a loud screech.

The Witch turned to see it pounce upon her. She screamed and it exploded into chunks of bone and blood, coating her in effluence that sizzled and boiled upon its touch.

The Witch turned back around to face Janet, a trickle of blood dribbled from her mouth and the red glow began to dim. Janet looked to the Witches naked chest and saw that a rib bone from the exploded creature had pierced the flesh between her breasts.

"It's, in my heart. Ha, well. Goodbye, Janet. Nice meeting you, I guess," she said, becoming unconscious and falling several feet to the floor.

The church snapped back into normality as if waking from a dream as the Glitterwitch died.

Janet fainted out of hunger and stress. Her head cracking on the cobblestones of the church.

She woke up several hours later in a puddle of her own blood. Janet's head ached and darkness flooded the church. She thought herself dead at first but she managed to stand up, feeling her way forwards she managed to stumble over the bodies of Slice, the Blobwoman and the Glitterwitch in the darkness. Feeling for the oak door which was wide open she then stepped outside.

Her eyes adjusted to the dim light coming from the cloudy covered moon. The sea was gone, in place vast desert stretched into infinity. She could see thin spectres climbing out of the ground and marching towards her. She stood and waited for them to come to her.

After an hour, a million naked beautiful people had surrounded the church and they watched Janet silently. Janet didn't say anything. Too scared to move, she watched them expecting them to rip her to bits like they did with the dragon.

After ten minutes of this, the naked people got bored and began to move on. Slowly moving off into the desert, the only sound they made being their footsteps in the white sand. When the last had left the church, Janet, still naked and afraid, went to follow them.

She quickly glimpsed her reflection in one of the stained glass windows. Janet was thin and beautiful. A thought popped into her head. She was no longer hungry and scared, she was almost happy. Smiling to herself Janet turned and ran towards the other beautiful people.

Janet would never be alone again.

ABOUT THE AUTHOR

Leigham Shardlow Lives!

Printed in Great Britain
by Amazon

24201438R00067